To Megan, Broo...

The ELFLING PRINCESS

**Story & Illustrations
by Cheryl Kaye Tardif**

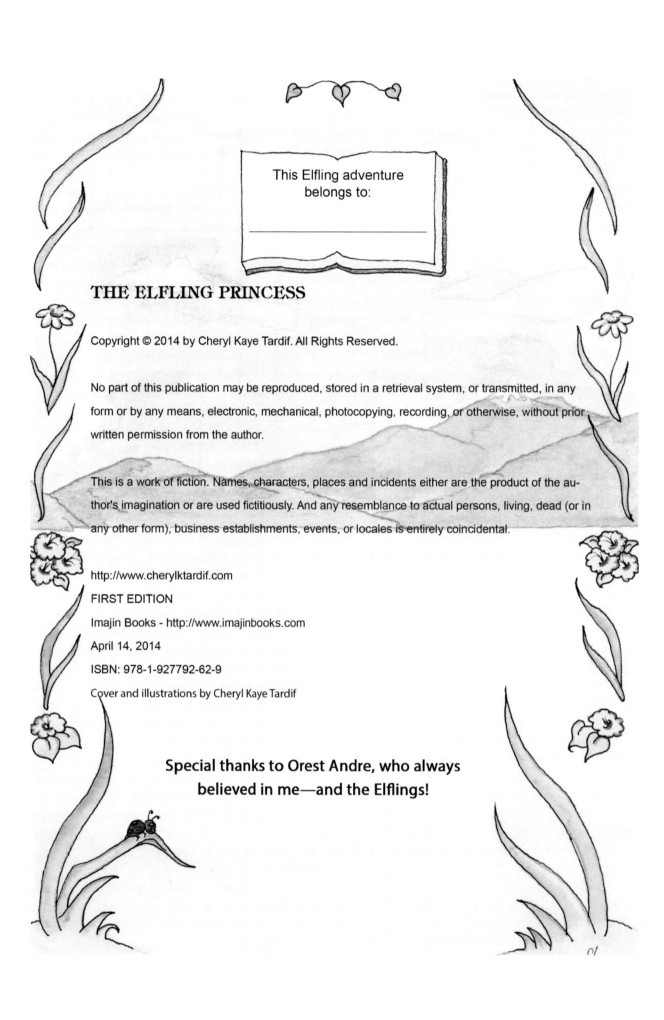

This Elfling adventure
belongs to:

_____

THE ELFLING PRINCESS

http://www.cherylktardif.com

FIRST EDITION

Imajin Books - http://www.imajinbooks.com

April 14, 2014

ISBN: 978-1-927792-62-9

Cover and illustrations by Cheryl Kaye Tardif

Special thanks to Orest Andre, who always believed in me—and the Elflings!

For my angels—Jessica and Sebastien

Once upon a time, in a world full of magic, there was a kingdom that only few humans had ever seen—the Elfling Kingdom.

Elflings are tiny creatures, the children of the world's first elves. They have pointed ears and hair that is a darker shade than their skin. Their bodies glow any color you can imagine. Elfling girls have silvery wings that shine like satin spider webs. Very few Elfling boys have wings, so they must fly on the backs of birds. But if they are small enough, their sisters will piggy-back them.

Have you ever seen an Elfling?

I know a golden-haired girl named Jessica, who met some Elflings while playing behind her house with her brother, Sebastien. This is her story.

So close your eyes, and I'll tell you all about Jessica, Sebastien and the search for the Elfling Princess...

1

It was a beautiful, sunny day. The birds were singing, the flowers were blooming and the water was warm. A herd of pink unicorns danced in the meadow...

"What are you day-dreaming about this time?" Jessica's mother asked.

Jessica smiled as her imaginary unicorns disappeared. "Nothing, Mom."

"Why don't you go play with your brother?" Mom suggested.

Jessica and her brother, Sebastien, tossed a red and blue beach ball back and forth.

When Sebastien ran behind a tree, Jessica tried to catch him and tripped over a log. The ball flew out of her hands.

"Where did it go?" Jessica asked her brother.

They looked everywhere—under a picnic table, in the bushes and behind the log, but the ball was gone.

Your ball is in the tree branch," someone squeaked.

Sebastien looked at his sister. "How will we get it down?"

Jessica thought about this, waiting for an answer. The park grew silent, as if it too were waiting.

Almost as though a magic wand had been waved, the ball slowly floated to the ground.

"Where did that voice come from?" Jessica asked.

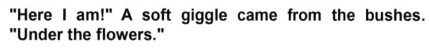

"Here I am!" A soft giggle came from the bushes. "Under the flowers."

The children were amazed to find a glowing girl hiding under a patch of daisies. She had long white hair, pointed ears and shiny wings on her back.

"Don't be afraid," the strange girl said. "My name is Malaya. I am an Elfling."

She flew over to a pink rosebud and sat down.

"I'm trying to find the Elfling Princess," she whispered.

Malaya held out her hands and a tiny golden book appeared.

"No one knows what she looks like," the Elfling said sadly. "The Book of Wonders says that, unless I find her, our Kingdom will be destroyed by an evil monster."

"I'll help you look," Jessica said. "Sebastien, bring the ball back home."

While Malaya flew off towards a hill, Jessica followed the babbling brook until she came to a small clearing just behind her house. In front of her stood the tallest tree she had ever seen.

Tired, she lay beneath the tree and closed her eyes. She imagined a dragon dragonfly, a butterfly and bee dancing, and a turtle and mouse playing cards.

"Ouch!" She scowled as a berry hit her forehead.

"Got her!" giggled a voice from above.

Jessica looked up and saw two Elfling boys sitting on the branch and an Elfling girl floating nearby. They all glowed softly—mauve, green and blue.

Just then, something moved in the bushes behind the tree. Was it a huge animal? Maybe it was a terrible monster looking for something tasty to eat.

Suddenly, Sebastien's head appeared.

"Look!" Jessica said, pointing to the tree branch. "I found more Elflings."

"How do you know about us?" the oldest of the Elfling boys demanded.

"Shh, Torag! We must not talk to humans or else they will turn us to stone," the girl said fearfully.

"That's just a Human-Tale, Meesha," Torag scowled. "I'm not afraid."

He took a few steps forward.

"Oops! Help, I'm falling!" Torag yelled as he slipped off the branch. Down, down he fell.

Splat! Torag landed safely in Jessica's hand.

"Who are you two?" he asked in a grumpy voice.

"We are friends, Torag," both children replied.

"This is my sister, Meesha, and my brother, Noma," Torag pointed.

Noma smiled at Sebastien shyly while Meesha waited to be turned to stone.

The children told the Elflings about meeting Malaya and of the search for the Elfling Princess.

"It's too late," Noma spoke up. "Malaya has already returned to our Kingdom and told the Elf King she had failed. Then she disappeared into the forest.

"We can help you find her," Jessica smiled. "After all, this is our back yard."

Suddenly, the park grew dark and quiet. The birds stopped singing and the brook stopped babbling.

"It's the Book of Wonders!" the Elflings cried.

A bald eagle heard Torag's silent call and swept him up on its back.

The children followed Meesha's glittery trail.

Meesha warned them that if the last page of the Book of Wonders turned, the evil monster would destroy the Elfling Kingdom.

Only the Elfling Princess could save them.

When they reached a rocky hill, Torag pointed.

Hundreds of glowing Elflings circled around an old tree stump. Their bodies gleamed softly, rainbow colors.

It was the Book of Wonders—only bigger this time.

Its pages were turning as if someone was reading its mysteries. As each page turned, the Elflings gasped in dismay.

Soon, there were only six pages left.

Torag closed his eyes, no longer the tough guy.

The Book of Wonders spoke, "The Elfling Kingdom is doomed because there is no leader to help you. The Elfling Princess can be your leader and save you from the monster."

"What is this monster called?" Torag asked.

"It is called Forgetfulness," the Book answered.

Only three pages were left.

It continued, "For centuries the Elflings have been part of Human stories, but now the humans have forgotten how to dream. If this magic dies, the Humans will also die, for it is the magic of Imagination that keeps us all alive."

"I want to help," Jessica spoke up, "but how do we find the Elfling Princess?"

"Sometimes what we are looking for is right under our nose." The Book closed, never turning its last page.

"The Princess is already here—she just needs to believe in herself."

"But where is the Elfling Princess?" Sebastien asked.

"Jessica, you are the Elfling Princess," the book answered. "You have the gift of Imagination."

"Me?" Jessica's mouth hung open in disbelief.

"You must always believe in the magic of the Elflings, so that we will never be forgotten," Meesha begged, landing on Jessica's shoulder.

As the Book of Wonders disappeared, a light swirled around Jessica.

"I will never forget the Elflings," she promised.

Immediately, the sun chased all the dark clouds away, except one.

"It's the Elf King!" the Elflings shouted excitedly.

"It is just a cloud," Jessica giggled.

"Use the magic," Meesha replied.

And magically, the cloud became a cloud castle.

"You must be Jessica, the Elfling Princess," the Elf King said. The wispy, old Elf was made entirely from cloud puffs, except his crown and staff.

"Please look after our Elflings," he continued. "They can be a lazy bunch. Perhaps you can find them something important to do."

The Elf King leaned forward and blew two kisses, one for each of the Human children.

"Now," he began, "everyone who sees these marks will know that Jessica is the Elfling Princess, and Sebastien is the Prince of Hope."

Everyone watched as the Elf King and the cloud castle folded up and floated away.

Jessica and Sebastien followed their Elfling friends across the babbling brook, which was once again babbling, and towards their house.

"How will you know which job to give us?" Torag pouted, before flying away.

"We'll use the magic—our Imaginations," Jessica shouted as the Elflings disappeared into the trees.

"Where have you two been?" Mother asked curiously.

"You'll never guess!" Sebastien exclaimed. "We met the Elflings, a talking book that flies, the Elf King and—"

Mother shook her head, laughing. "What did you really do today?" she asked. "Did you meet any other children in the park?"

Jessica smiled a mysterious smile. "Yes, Mother," she answered, "we met lots of children today."

Jessica winked at Sebastien. He laughed and winked back at his sister, the Elfling Princess.

And Jessica was not telling a lie, was she? They had met lots of children—Elfling children.

So now you know how Jessica became the Elfling Princess.

I bet you are wondering if they find Malaya, and which job Torag gets. Well, you will have to use the greatest gift you have been given—the magic of Imagination—because that is another story!

THE END

About the Author

Cheryl Kaye Tardif is an award-winning, international bestselling Canadian suspense author. She wrote and illustrated this story when her daughter, Jessica, was very young, but it was never published until now. Cheryl brought *The Elfling Princess* to schools and daycares and read it to the children. It was very well received, inspiring such comments from the kids as: "I saw an Elfling last night!" and "I saw one in my bedroom!"

Cheryl is now working on her next thriller. However, she does have one final children's book she plans to publish next year.

Booklist raves, "Tardif, already a big hit in Canada…a name to reckon with south of the border."

Cheryl's website: http://www.cherylktardif.com
Official blog: http://www.cherylktardif.blogspot.com
Twitter: http://www.twitter.com/cherylktardif
Facebook: https://www.facebook.com/pages/Cheryl-Kaye-Tardif-novels/29769736630

You can also find Cheryl Kaye Tardif on Goodreads, Shelfari and LibraryThing, plus other social networks.

IMAJIN BOOKS

Quality fiction beyond your wildest dreams

For your next eBook or paperback purchase, please visit:

www.imajinbooks.com

www.twitter.com/imajinbooks

www.facebook.com/imajinbooks